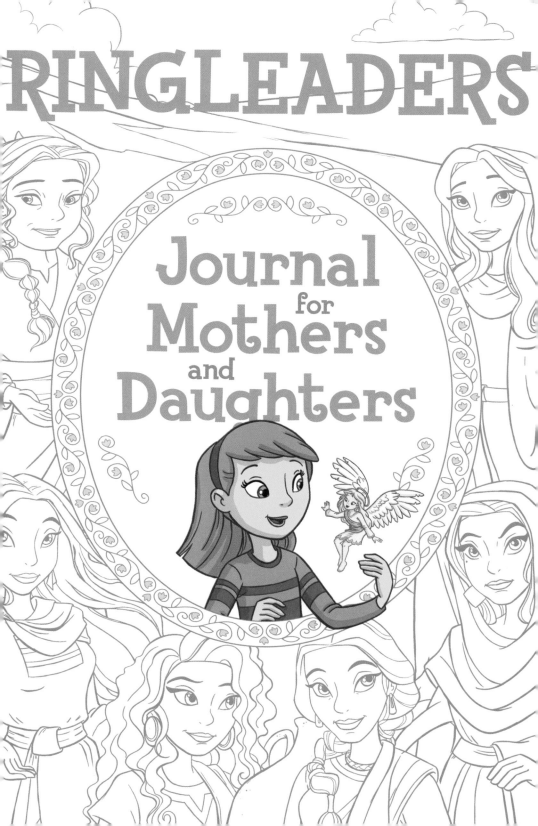

RINGLEADERS

Journal
for
Mothers
and
Daughters

Text © 2020 by Erin Weidemann

Interior Design by: John Trent
Cover Design by: John Trent
Character Illustrations by: Megan Crisp

Manufactured in the United States

978-1-7354611-1-3

BibleBelles.com

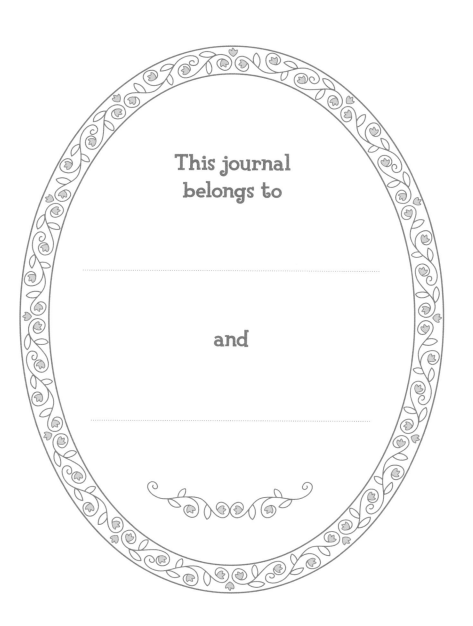

This journal
belongs to

....

and

....

You Have A Powerful Voice.

Welcome to the Ringleaders Journal. This interactive journal is the perfect compliment to the Bible Belles® Ringleaders collection and devotional. Inside, you will find fun ways to dive deeper into the stories of the Ringleaders—Elizabeth, Mary, the Samaritan woman, Mary and Martha, and Mary Magdalene—and celebrate the unique role each of them played in God's great rescue plan. You've got a unique role to play too. You can learn to use your voice for God and for good.

This journal offers a safe place for you to share feelings, thoughts, and ideas and gives you space to be open and honest as you and your mom pursue growth and a stronger connection . . . together. It includes writing prompts and verses, as well as free space to record whatever comes to mind.

As you make your way through these pages, my prayer is that God would use the gospel to stir both of your spirits and align your hearts with His heart as you to think up creative ways to share the Good News with others. That's what being a Ringleader is all about.

Happy journaling!

Erin Weidemann

Table of Contents

Elizabeth

What I love most about the story of Elizabeth

mother

12

My favorite part of Elizabeth's story

daughter

mother

My favorite scene

daughter

free space

free space

free space

free space

Elizabeth's story is important because

_____

_____

_____

_____

_____

_____

_____

mother

A time when I struggled to choose joy over jealousy

_____

_____

_____

_____

_____

_____

_____

_____

_____

_____

What Elizabeth's story shows me

What I can do when I feel disappointed

daughter

Something miraculous God has done in my life

Something miraculous God has done in my life

daughter

free space

free space

Free space

free space

How I know God is at work in my life

mother

Like Elizabeth, I can be

daughter

Let us hold unswervingly to the hope we profess,
for he who promised is faithful. – Hebrews 10:23

What does *holding unswervingly to the hope we profess* mean to us?

mother + daughter

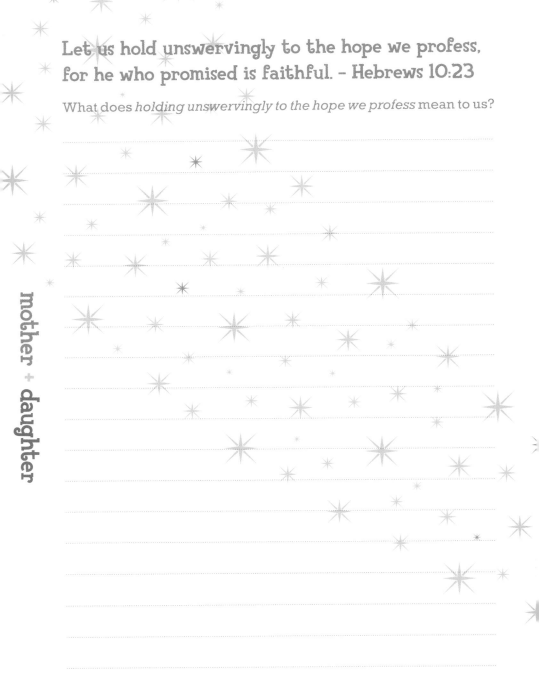

What can we do to encourage each other to keep the faith during hard times?

mother + daughter

free space

free space

33

free space

He turns
her darkness
into light.

Mary

Why Mary is a hero of mine

mother

What I learn from Mary

daughter

The scene I like best

mother

My favorite scene

daughter

free space

free space

free space

free space

Mary's story is important because

....
....
....
....
....
....
....
....

mother

Times I have struggled with obedience

....
....
....
....
....
....
....
....
....
....

What I love most about Mary

....
....
....
....
....
....
....

Times I have struggled with obedience

....
....
....
....
....
....
....
....

daughter

Why obeying God is so hard for me sometimes

How I feel when I'm being told what to do

daughter

free space

free space

53

free space

free space

What I need to remember about listening to and doing what God says

What I need to do to say, "Yes" to God more in my life

daughter

I desire to do your will, my God; your law is within my heart. – Psalm 40:8

What do we think *doing God's will* means?

mother + daughter

What are some ways we can encourage each other to keep his law within our hearts?

mother + daughter

free space

free space

free space

free space

He keeps her
in perfect
peace.

#ADifferentKindOfNoise

The Samaritan Woman

What I learn from the story of the Samaritan Woman

mother

My favorite part of the story

daughter

The scene I like best

mother

My favorite scene

daughter

free space

free space

free space

free space

A time when I felt unloved

What I believe this story can teach us

A time when I felt unloved

I feel most loved when

daughter

Why simply talking to Jesus helps me

mother

What I can tell myself the next time I feel left out

daughter

free space

free space

Free space

free space

83

Why it's important to share Jesus like the Samaritan Woman did

mother

What I can do to tell people about Him

So is my word that goes out from my mouth:
It will not return to me empty, but will
accomplish what I desire and achieve the
purpose for which I sent it. - Isaiah 55:11

What does it mean that God's word will not return to Him empty?

mother + daughter

What are some ways we can send His word out into the world?

mother + daughter

free space

free space

free space

She loves
with servant
hands and a
humble heart.

Mary and Martha

Why the story of Mary and Martha is important to me

mother

What I like best about this story

daughter

The scene I like best

mother

My favorite part of the story

daughter

free space

free space

free space

free space

What the story teaches me about spending time with God

....

....

....

....

....

....

....

A time in my life when I felt like God was far away

....

....

....

....

....

....

....

....

....

mother

What I normally do when I'm worried about something

What I can do instead

daughter

105

What I've learned over the years about spending time with God

Where and when it is easiest for me to sit, listen, and hear from God

daughter

What I do to focus my time and thoughts on God

mother

What would make my quiet time with God really special

daughter

free space

Free space

free space

113

Blessed is the one who does not walk in step with the wicked or stand in the way that sinners take or sit in the company of mockers, but whose delight is in the law of the Lord, and who meditates on his law day and night. That person is like a tree planted by streams of water which yields its fruit in season and whose leaf does not wither—whatever they do prospers. – Psalm 1:1-3

How can we be women whose *delight is in the law of the Lord?*

How can we encourage each other to meditate on his law day and night?

free space

free space

117

free space

free space

Under his wings
she finds
her refuge.

Mary Magdalene

Why Mary Magdalene's story is important for me

mother

What I like best about Mary Magdalene

daughter

My favorite scene from her story

The scene I like best

daughter

free space

free space

free space

free space

Why Mary Magdalene is an example of a faith-filled leader

How I feel about my own ability to share the gospel

Like Mary Magdalene, I can share Jesus by

....

....

....

....

....

....

....

What I think it means to follow Jesus

....

....

....

....

....

....

....

....

daughter

Someone whose faith inspires me

Someone whose faith inspires me

daughter

free space

free space

Free space

free space

My dreams for my daughter's faith

mother

What my mom has taught me about following Jesus

daughter

Sing to the Lord a new song; sing to the Lord, all the earth. Sing to the Lord, praise his name; proclaim his salvation day after day. Declare his glory among the nations, his marvelous deeds among all peoples. – Psalm 96:1-3

What does it mean to us to *proclaim his salvation day after day?*

What are some ways we can work together to tell others what God has done?

free space

free space

free space

What I've learned from this journal and our time writing in it

mother

What I've learned from this journal and our time writing in it

daughter

free space

free space

free space

free space

free space

free space

She smiles
because she
is free.